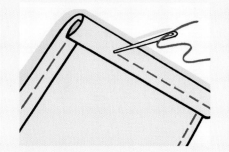

1 Cut a rectangle of fabric to match your measurements (see left). Make sure one of the sides lines up with the true edge and keep the other edges in line with it.

2 Fold over 1cm down both side edges and then 1cm again. Ask a grown-up to crease the folds with an iron. Stitch the foldovers with an in-and-out stitch or ask a grown-up to machine them. Do the same for the top and bottom edges.

3 Prepare to print: protect your working area with scrap paper, and pour your fabric paints onto flat plates. Prepare printing blocks such as cookie cutters and short pieces of dowel. Fold strips of card lengthways and curl them into shapes that you print with the folded edges.

4 Practise printing on scrap fabric or paper. Dab the printing block in the paint, blot, and print. When you have a design you like, spread your apron fabric out smooth and flat and print on it.

5 Cut two 50cm lengths of stout cotton tape for the shoulder straps. Safety pin in place at the front, then ask a helper to pin the left front tape to the right back edge and the right front tape to the left back edge so that it fits you.

6 Remove the apron and adjust the straps, checking they are the same length and not twisted. Trim off any extra length. Then stitch strongly in place.

• REDUCE... wear on your clothes

• REUSE... your apron for ever-grubbier jobs, and finally use it as rags for cleaning

• RECYCLE... larger pieces of fabric from sheets or grown-up sized shirts

Use decorative stitching and button trims when you attach the straps. Wear the apron with the straps crossing over at the back.

2 Green party

When lots of friends come to a party, you need lots of tableware. Here are ideas for how to set a festive table without buying loads of disposables.

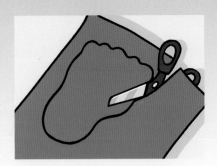

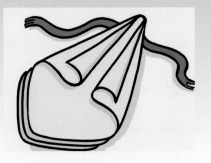

1 Make two tags for each guest from natural paper. Choose your own shape or copy the footprint template.

2 In contrasting paper, cut the shape of the inner sole and five toes for each shape. Stick these on. Then punch the hole and loop in a tie. Add the name of the guest.

3 Choose fabric napkins. Fold each napkin in half and half again, then gather and tie as shown. Arrange the folds neatly.

Cut or punch paper shapes from oddments of your party paper to use as table confetti.

4 Collect small glass bottles and wash them carefully in hot water. Tie a named tag to each bottle so every guest knows which is theirs. Add drinking straws if you wish.

Jac

The Good Green Footprint

Words and crafts by Christina Goodings

Photography by John Williams

Illustration by Richard Deverell

Contents

I Clean green apron

Protect your good clothes with this simple apron. Wear it for all kinds of make-and-do projects.

Choose a sturdy woven fabric. Then ask a grown-up to help you find a true edge – either the selvedge or an edge made by ripping across the weave.

Next, ask someone to help you measure your waist and then take 10cm off the number and note it (e.g. 62cm waist less 10cm is 52cm). Then have them measure from just below your neck to your knee and note the number. These are the width and length of your rectangle.

Why not cut the basic shape of the tags in advance and have your friends personalize theirs as they arrive?

• REUSE... fabric napkins. Regularly washed and line-dried, they will last years.
• RECYCLE... If you need extra plates for a party, collect food packaging containers that can be washed and reused, before recycling in the usual way.

Tom

Jules

Sarah

3 Butterflies

Make these bright butterflies as a party activity… or make a splendid one to give as a gift.

Butterflies hold neatly torn scraps of paper as instant notebooks for taking messages or writing shopping lists.

1 Choose thin card for the wings, almost as tall as your peg and twice as wide. Fold it in half and draw a wing shape. Cut it out.

2 Unfold the wing and decorate with punched or cut-out paper shapes. Glue the wing to the peg.

3 Draw a body shape about the same size as your peg and cut it out. Add features with crayons or markers. Glue this on top of the wing.

• REDUCE…
your use of new paper for quick notes

4 Fair food favours

A sweet treat makes a great party favour – and provides your guests with natural energy to power their walking and cycling!

Ask a grown-up before you do any cooking, and wash your hands.

Note that the dough needs to be made the day before you bake it.

Fair trade foodstuffs give the food producers a living wage.

Look out for fair trade cocoa.

1 Measure into a bowl 150g softened butter, 100g soft brown sugar and 75g caster sugar. Mix together until light and creamy. Then ask a grown-up to help you add two eggs, one at a time. Add a spoonful of flour if needed to help the mixture stay smooth.

2 Now divide the mix into two. Sift into one bowl 175g self-raising flour and 1 teaspoon of vanilla essence. Mix well. Sift into the other bowl 150g self-raising flour and 1 tablespoon of cocoa. Mix.

3 Place baking parchment on your work surface. Roll out the vanilla dough to a rectangle about 30cm x 15cm and 3mm thick. Do the same with the chocolate dough. Slide the chocolate dough onto the vanilla dough and roll up together. Wrap in the parchment and chill overnight in the refrigerator.

Wrap cookies in natural cellophane and string to give to your guests.

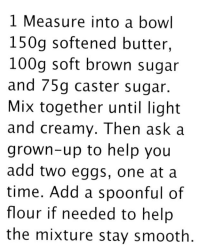

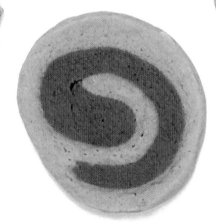

4 When you are ready to bake the cookies, ask a grown-up to heat the oven to 180°C. Line a baking tray with parchment. Unwrap your dough and slice into cookies about 5mm thick. Bake for 8 minutes. Ask a grown-up to lift the tray out of the oven and leave the cookies to cool.

• REDUCE... the number of throwaway trinkets you buy as party gifts

5 Little gift bag

These little bags are great for all kinds of gifts and also for party bags. You can make party bags ahead of time – or simply get the paper ready for your friends to make their own.

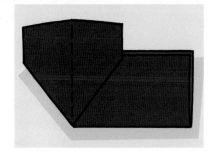

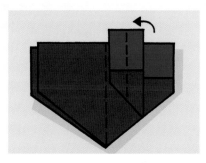

1 Take a rectangle of paper. A4 size makes a small but useful bag that is a good size to practice with. Fold the paper vertically right to left. Next fold it horizontally bottom to top.

2 Turn the paper with the long fold edge towards you and the short on the left. Lift the top flap up, and then squash it open as shown so the central crease lines up with the folded edge. Turn the piece over and squash the other flap to match.

3 Now fold the flap on the right so the right edge goes to the centre. Crease. Then take the folded right edge and fold that to the centre. Now do the same on the left. Then fold the top part down in line with the horizontal edge.

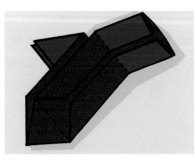

4 Turn over and repeat step 3 for the other side. Fold the lower triangle up, crease and unfold. Use your fingers to gently open the bag and flatten the base.

• REUSE... you can make small bags with leftover oddments or good bits of used wrapping paper
• RECYCLE... uncoated paper can be composted; many other types of paper can be recycled

To fasten the bag, lift
the top flaps and punch
through all thicknesses
on both left and right.
Thread a loop of string or
ribbon to close the bag.

6 Papier mâché pals

Papier mâché is a traditional craft that directly recycles non-glossy paper. Unwanted newspapers and thrown-out photocopies can all be used.

Make your glue from flour and water mixed till it is a bit like pouring cream, or from thinned PVA glue.

Prepare this project by tearing your paper into strips about 2cm wide and 5cm long. Tear lots!

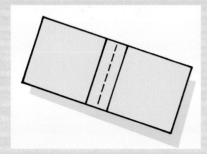

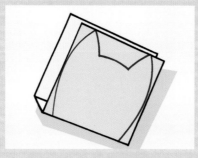

1 Start with a piece of thin card about 20cm x 30cm, perhaps cut from a cereal box. Mark the centre line at 15cm, and then lines 1cm away to left and right. Fold along these two lines to make a base, then unfold.

2 Draw your pal on one face of the card, giving it cute ear shapes. Cut out the shape, and cut the back to match.

3 Lightly tape the sides using strips of paper brushed with glue to make an open box. Insert a balloon and inflate it just enough to make the box bulge slightly so your pal is pleasingly plump.

4 To make sticky-out eyes, cut two eye-sized circles of thin card and two slightly smaller ones of thicker card. Glue the smaller ones on the bigger ones, then glue the bigger side to your pal.

5 Brush glue onto strips of paper and stick them all over your pal, leaving just the top open. Leave to dry (this may take overnight) and then add another layer.

6 When the glue is dry, paint your pal all over with gesso. Then use colourful paint to decorate. Remember to pop the balloon!

Your pal could be a money box or, with just a few coins for weight at the bottom, a pencil holder.

• REUSE... once-used paper
• RECYCLE... papier mâché in the same way as paper

7 On your bike

Travelling by car burns fuel. If your car burns petrol or diesel, the fuel gives off planet-harming emissions. One of these is carbon dioxide, which leads to global warming.

The only fuel needed for going on foot or by bike is food to give you energy. It's good for the planet and for you!

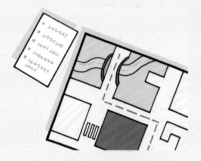

1 List all the places near enough to your home for you to reach by walking or cycling. Outline the roads, tracks, and pathways you will use to get there. Look at a map or aerial photograph to help you get the shape.

If you are cycling, be sure your bike is safely maintained and that you can start, ride, and stop confidently. Wear a helmet to protect your head against falls. Avoid roads with traffic unless you are with a responsible adult.

Ask a grown-up in your family to help you choose your routes. It is important to follow their advice on where is safe to go – especially using roads and crossing roads.

2 Draw little pictures or symbols of your house and the places you go to. Then draw landmarks of the places that help you know where you are. Stick on to your map.

- REDUCE... the amount you travel by car
- REUSE... consider using a second-hand bike
- RECYCLE... pass your outgrown bike to someone else

8 Green laundry

Scientists are working on all kinds of ways to make the most of solar energy and wind energy.

Use both directly by hanging clothes on an outside line to dry, and keep the pegs in this kite-shaped bag.

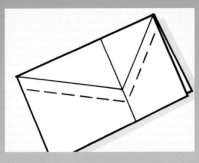

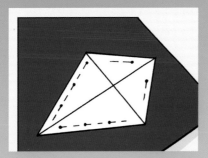

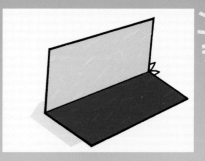

1 Take a rectangle of paper 60cm x 40cm and fold it in half lengthways. Draw half a kite shape, then add 2cm all round. Cut out the pattern and fold it from side point to side point.

2 Lay this pattern piece on the kite fabric you have chosen for the back. Ask a grown-up to help you check that the side-to-side crease is in line with a true edge of the fabric (see page 1). Pin the pattern in place and cut the fabric shape for the back. Unpin.

3 Prepare the front fabric: choose two strips of cloth 30cm x 40cm with a true edge in the centre. Ask a grown-up to machine these together. If this is a bother, a plain kite is nice too.

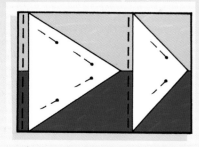

4 Fold your paper pattern on the side-to-side crease and cut. Pin both triangles to the front fabric with the points along the join and facing the same way as shown. Draw a pencil line 2cm away from the base of each to allow for turning. Cut out.

5 Fold over the 2cm you added for a turning to the two front pieces. Stitch the longer one (the bottom piece) from edge to edge. Stitch the upper one from the edge only part way across.

6 Then lay the front pieces on the back, right sides together. Stitch all round.

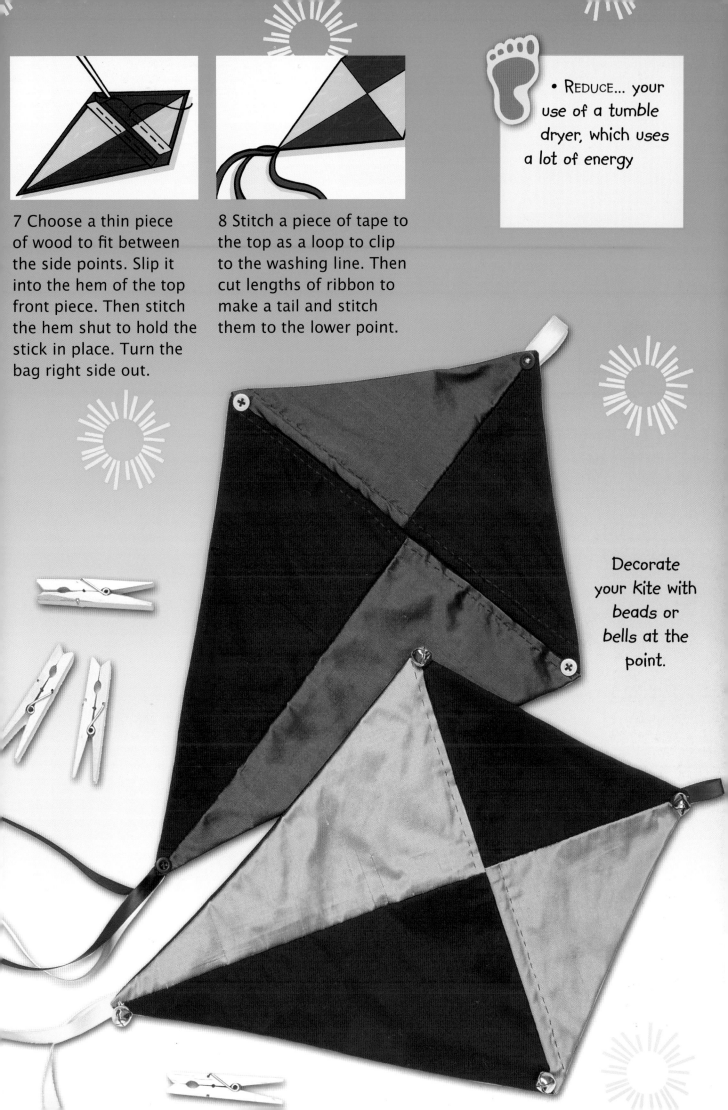

7 Choose a thin piece of wood to fit between the side points. Slip it into the hem of the top front piece. Then stitch the hem shut to hold the stick in place. Turn the bag right side out.

8 Stitch a piece of tape to the top as a loop to clip to the washing line. Then cut lengths of ribbon to make a tail and stitch them to the lower point.

• REDUCE... your use of a tumble dryer, which uses a lot of energy

Decorate your kite with beads or bells at the point.

9 Waste bin

Make a waste bin of… waste.

Eco-friendly wallpaper paste would be excellent for this craft, but PVA works well too. PVA also makes a good wipeable finish.

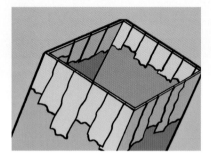

1 Choose a sturdy cardboard box, or ask a grown-up to help you cut one to the size and shape you want. Glue brown paper over any joins and any cut edges at the top.

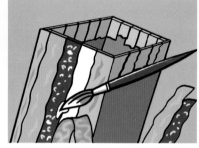

2 Tear scrap paper into long strips. A confident rip along the grain of the paper will be straight enough. Glue the strips down the side of the box, mixing light and dark shades to suit.

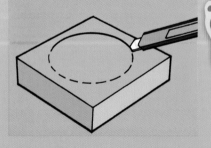

3 If you wish, ask a grown-up to help you cut a shallow box into a lid. Cut a hole in the top of the lid so you can "post" your rubbish through. Decorate to match the box.

• REDUCE… your use of plastic liners for rubbish. Use large paper envelopes or old cartons inside your splendid handmade bin.

10 Door hen

Be careful with the amount of energy you use to heat your home. Sometimes that will mean keeping some doors shut so as not to let the heat out. Sometimes it will mean propping them open so warm air (or a cool breeze) can circulate.

Door hen will keep a door in place.

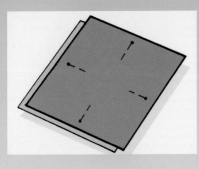

1 Cut two squares of felt. A good size is 20cm x 20cm. Mark the centre point of each side of one of the squares with a pin.

2 Use the templates to cut two tail pieces, two left wings and two right wings (or make up your own shapes). Use contrasting colours if you like. Stitch each pair of pieces together with bright stitches.

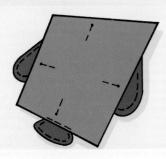

3 Now centre the wing and tail pieces on the underside of the marked square. Pin in place with a 1cm underlap and lightly stitch in place with thread you will later remove.

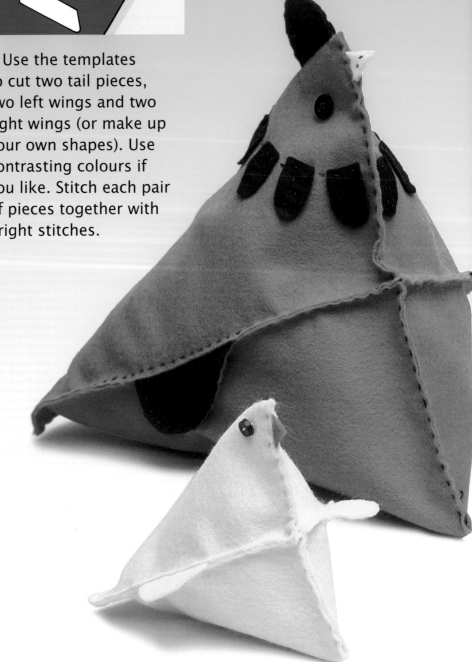

 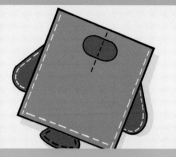 

4 Stitch the top and bottom square together through all thicknesses on three sides.

If you wish, cut neck "feathers" and stitch them onto the top piece at the same time as step 3.

5 Cut a comb piece, and leave it unfolded. Centre it on the fourth pin marker of the upper square and stitch it to the felt, then fold it together and stitch through both edges. Add button eyes.

6 Your hen is now like an empty bag. Pull the comb up so the seamed sides come together and pin this fourth seam.

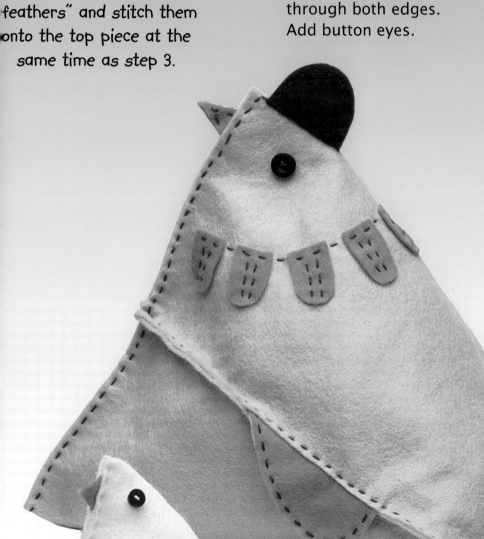

7 Cut a beak piece and stitch it in place as you stitch the fourth seam. Before you reach the end, fill the hen with beans or marbles. Finish the seam. Remove any temporary stitching.

• REDUCE... the number of rooms you keep warm when no one is in them

11 Personal insulation

If you walk and cycle in cooler weather, you need to insulate yourself from the weather.

   Find out just how much difference it makes to insulate yourself. As well as staying warmer, you will better understand the importance of insulating a home!

1 Measure round your head. Now cut a rectangle of fleece a little smaller than this wide and about 35cm high. Hold it round you head and trim a little smaller in width if you need to.

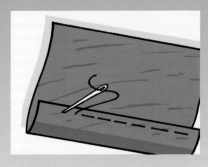

2 Fold one of the long edges up about 6cm. Stitch in place with bright thread.

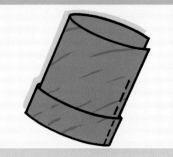

3 Now stitch the short sides together from the lower edge to about 5cm from the top. Fold your tube flat so the seam is at the centre back and pin the top edge.

4 Check the fit and decide where to put the top line of stitches. Then stitch the hat, leaving about 5cm above the lines of stitching. Add beads or buttons as extra trim.

5 Ask a grown-up to help you snip the top into a fringe. Wild, but warm.

- REDUCE... the amount of time you spend in heated vehicles
- REUSE... a worn-out fleece as a hat
- RECYCLE... plastic bottles to make more polyester fleece (really!)

You can cut a length of fleece to make a scarf and fringe it in the same way.

12 Everything bag

Here is a clever way to turn a metre square of fabric into a bag.
It works best with not-too-thick fabrics.

This bag uses cheap decorators' cotton printed with fabric paints.
Begin by cutting a metre square of fabric. Double fold the edges
and stitch them.

1 Prepare to print,
protecting your working
area with scrap paper.
Lay the metre square out
flat. Put fabric paint on
a flat plate. Collect the
bottles you want to print
with.

2 Dip a bottle in the
paint, blot on paper and
practise printing. Use the
base and the neck to give
different sized circles.
When you are happy with
the effect, print your
fabric. Leave it to dry.

3 Fold the square into
a triangle. Take the two
side points and knot
them about a third of
the way in.

4 Turn the side knots
in. Tie the top points to
make a handle.

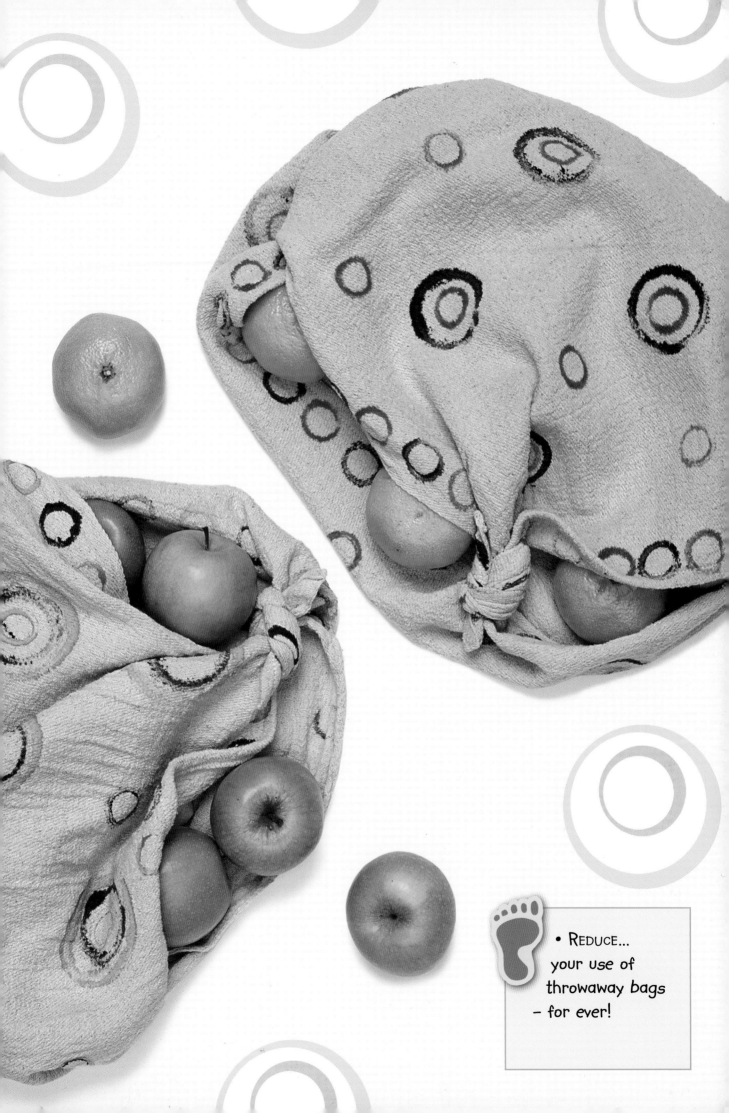

• REDUCE...
your use of
throwaway bags
– for ever!

13 Anything soup (almost!)

This vegetable soup – a bit like minestrone – really needs an onion and a can of tomatoes (or about 500g of fresh tomatoes in season). The rest can be adjusted to use up whatever vegetables you have – and like!

Ask a grown-up before you start cooking. Wash your hands and wear an apron.

Serve the soup with bread, or pour some over a plateful of boiled rice.

1 Carefully peel an onion and ask a grown-up to help you chop it carefully. Find a bowl (or cup) that it will just fit into. Tip the onion back onto a plate.

2 Now chop four or five bowlfuls of other vegetables. Try one each of carrot, celery, potato, courgette, and green beans. If you don't have enough, add half a bowl of red lentils instead of fresh vegetable.

3 Heat a little oil in a casserole dish. Add the onion and stir over a low heat for three minutes. Then add the other vegetables one by one, stirring between each.

4 Add a can of tomatoes and stir, or chop 500g fresh tomatoes and add. Allow to cook for 5-8 minutes.

5 If the soup seems too thick, add a little water. Then add a little salt and pepper and let the soup simmer for about 20 minutes.

• REDUCE... the amount of food you throw away
• RECYCLE... vegetable peelings in the compost

14 Green prints

Make simple wrapping paper by printing brown or uncoated white paper.
   You don't have to stick to green.
   When using paint in this way, be sure to protect surfaces with plenty
of scrap paper.

1 Make a stringbottle
printing roller: tape
a length of thick but
smooth string to the
neck of your bottle then
wind it tightly round.
Tape the other end
down.

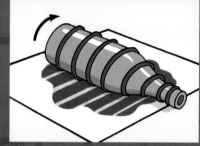

2 Spread your printing
ink onto a large tile and
roll your bottle on it,
or apply the ink to the
string with a printer's
roller.

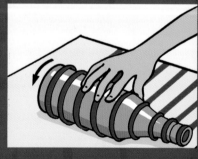

3 Choose the paper you
are going to print. Roll
the bottle over from
one side to the other,
pressing gently. Do
this all over the paper.
If you wish, repeat in a
crossways direction.

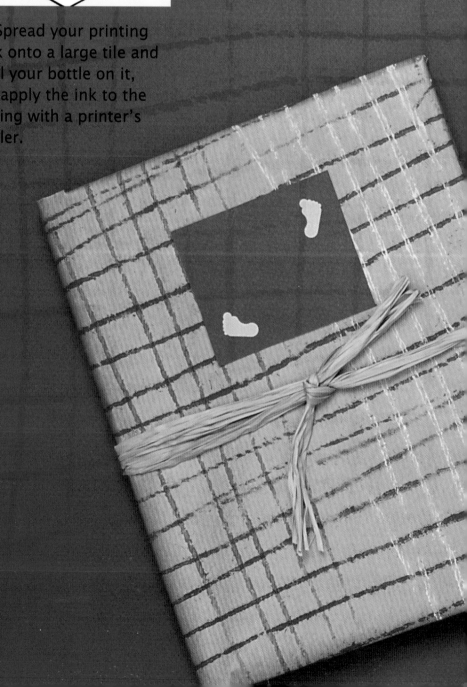

• REDUCE... your use of gift wrap, especially those with metallic finishes that don't decompose easily

This method quickly makes plain paper fabulous. Use it for gifts or for protecting much-read books. Use the other printing ideas on pages 1 and 12 for other designs.

15 Green, green glass

Glass can be recycled and made into new products.
However, that kind of recycling process takes a lot of energy.
Try finding new uses for jars and bottles in simpler ways.

1 Wash and dry your jar thoroughly. Wind strips of masking tape tightly around in bands, twisting the end to give a "bump". Then brush all over with gesso. When it is dry, add another coat.

2 Next, paint over the gesso with colour. Acrylic paints are the most hardwearing. Let the paint just dry, then unwind the tape slowly. Make good any bad tears.

- REDUCE... the number of things you buy in glass if there is a simpler alternative
- REUSE... glass just as it is when you can
- RECYCLE... glass in the proper bin

Glassware can become... a vase, a money bottle, a pencil holder, a gift jar to fill with sweets or homemade biscuits (like on page 4)...

16 Green-fingered genius

One of the best things you can do for a greener planet is to get gardening.

Even if you have very little space, a pot will do for a start. You might have a proper pot or simply ask a grown-up to help cut drainage holes in the base of an old bucket or plastic bottle. Fill it with soil and keep this moist and in a light place, preferably outdoors.

Plant seeds for vegetables or flowers, or even a tree.

Or leave your pot bare to see what wild plants blow in.

Wherever you find earth, do what you can to let it grow green.